W hat do you see when you look at me?" she said. It took Dave a few seconds to realize she was talking to him.

"A hippie," Dave said. "And a delusional one at that."

"So I'm no more than a label? And that's it? What about a fellow human in pain?"

"Fellow human?" Dave said. "No such thing. We're all just information that needs a bit of tweaking."

"Information? What am I… some kind of fucking computer?"

"Something like that," Dave said. He too was warming to the conversation now. It was taking a direction he could relate to.

"So you're a mechanist?" Maggie continued. "All human passion, all memory, all imagination…the complete human experience. All of it just comes from the chemistry in our brains…like the movements of a clock follow from the arrangement of its cogs and wheels?"

Dave nodded.

"Clockwork dolls, the lot of us."

CLOCKWORK DOLLS

WILLIAM MEIKLE

For friends and family, the only answer I need

Acknowledgments

Many thanks to the whole team at Crossroad Press who pulled this project together.

JUNE 11TH

D ave Burns sat with his head in his hands.

At least they've taken the cuffs off.

The police interview room was colder than the night outside; the chair he'd been dropped onto was barely functional, and the glass of water on the table in front of him looked like the last occupant had spat in it. The only light came from a stark neon bulb overhead that swung at the end of a fraying cord, just enough to be irritating.

But all in all, this is better than the alternative.

"Happy days," he whispered.

He sat on one side of a table that had a distinct lopsided slope to the left. Opposite him on the far side of the table sat a large, bored-looking cop. The cop noticed that Dave had looked up.

"Whenever you're ready, son," the big man said. "I'm listening."

"She meant the world to me," Dave said.

"Spare me the self-pitying crap. This is a murder inquiry, not a RELATE session," the cop replied.

"I loved her."

The cop laughed and leaned forward in his chair.

"You have no idea how many people have sat in that chair and said that," he said.

"But I meant it."

"They say that too. Being in love is no barrier to a murderous rage. But you know that already…don't you, Mr. Burns?"

1

"I'll be the first to admit that I know a bit more about rage than I'd like to. But I didn't kill anybody," Dave said. He heard the tremble in his voice. He didn't know whether the cop believed him.

Hell, I don't even know if I believe it myself.

"You'll have to prove that to me," the cop said.

"That's what I'm trying to do."

A car engine revved in the distance, and Dave jumped, almost falling out of his chair. The noise cut off as suddenly as it had come.

Dave eyed the corners warily.

Did that shadow just move?

"We might not have time," he said.

The cop interrupted him and sighed theatrically.

"I know, you told me already. Something big and bad is on its way." He waved his hands in the air and laughed. "Help me, the boogie man is coming. I'm so scared, I've *shit* myself."

Dave almost smiled, but humor was a long way off.

And might not be coming back.

"It doesn't really matter whether you believe me or not," Dave said. "The Cosmos doesn't care."

"What's all this *Cosmos* crap?"

Dave ignored the question and asked one of his own.

"Are you a religious man, officer?"

The cop smiled.

"Just a poor pilgrim trying to find his way."

"I don't understand that in a cop. Not with the things you must have seen. How can you believe in God when there are so many things wrong in the world and it is obvious that he doesn't care?"

The cop smiled again.

"The Bible says that God is love. And part of His loving nature is that He allows people to have free will. As a result, we have evil, pain and suffering, due to the choices we and others make."

"So I was right. He doesn't care?"

"Of course he cares. He sent his only son to die for us. That's how much he cares. He could intervene and control everything about our lives but then we would be just robots and not truly free."

"That's the bit I never got," Dave said. "He gives us free will. Then, when we use it, he punishes us for not doing what *he* wanted in the first place. That's not free will. That's tyranny."

The cop took him seriously enough to answer.

"God does not violate our wills by choosing us and redeeming us. Rather, He changes our hearts so that our wills choose Him," he said.

"So, if, to be saved by Christ, I must give up my free will, then do we truly have freedom? Is it really our choice to be saved if, in the end, we do not have the ability to choose salvation for ourselves?"

"I'll tell you what my priest told me," the cop replied. "When you accept Christ as offered in the gospel, you receive salvation by your own decision. As such, salvation is your work. *You* must initiate the act. But it is also God's work, for it is God who offers salvation to you. Without Christ, there is no salvation."

"So all I have to do is ask, and it shall be given?"

"If your heart is pure. Yes."

Dave laughed. It was almost a sob.

"Ah, there's the problem, right there."

"Look," the cop said. "Why don't we skip the philosophy and get on to the business end of things?"

"I'm getting there. Just let me tell it my way. It'll be faster."

Dave looked at the shadows in the corner once more before concentrating on the cop's face.

"Ask and it shall be given? That's what you said, right? Well, I've got a story for you.

"It started last month. Jane and Jim Barr invited me over to dinner. I almost turned them down, but any chance to see her was better than none at all.

"And I had to get drunk before I could even bring myself to look at them."

MAY 13TH

D ave was getting roaring drunk. He wasn't enjoying it, but
that wasn't the point. The point was that two of the other
three people in the room were his best friends, and they were
better than Dave; better at their jobs, better in their sex-lives, better
at *life*.

But I'm the better drunk.

The others around the table had made an effort and were
smartly dressed for dinner, but Dave had deliberately chosen a
tired and faded shirt. He had the sleeves rolled up to show his
skinny white forearms, and he wore a very old pair of denim
trousers that he'd owned since back in the day.

When I was the better man.

The remains of a large meal and a heavy drinking session were
strewn across the table, with most of the empty bottles within arm's
reach of Dave. He took another hefty swig of wine, then
remembered he was in the middle of a joke.

"So they find the clitoris is missing…it's been cut away." He
swilled more wine. "And the nurse says…" He paused, looking
around the table. Nobody seemed to care. Jim and Jane were bent
close, Jim whispering into Jane's ear.

In that case, I'll just have to speak louder.

"Go on guess what the nurse says…. Go on."

By now he was nearly shouting. But nobody answered him —
nobody even looked interested in answering. He was too far gone
to stop.

"She says…it can't have been a man then…he'd never have found it!" He laughed, too long, too loud, spraying a fine mist of wine down his shirt and slopping some out of his glass onto his jeans. "He'd never have found it!"

The other three looked weary and bored…not a single smile from any of them. There was a long, embarrassed pause that Dave pretended not to notice. After another large swig of wine, he plowed on. He'd come with the intention of saying what was on his mind, and the drink had now loosened his moral center enough to let it through the usual filters.

He turned so that he was looking straight at Jane. And if he held his glass up just right, he was almost able to blot Jim, her husband, out of his view all together.

"Do you remember Jane, that night in Miami, when the moonlight played on the sea and we slept on the beach? We didn't have a stitch on and…"

He was *almost* pleased to see Jane look embarrassed. Beside her, and directly across the table from Dave, Jim Barr, Jane's husband went red in the face, but it wasn't embarrassment. This was impending rage.

"Why do you always have to be such an asshole, Dave?"

Jim looked to Dave's right, addressing the woman that sat there. Dave had been studiously ignoring her since he sat down to dinner, and couldn't even remember her name.

"He's always been like this, Maggie…even when we were students."

Dave finally turned to look at the woman the others had deemed would be his *date* for the night. She was actually very pretty in a kind of hippy-goth type way, but he wasn't in any mood to be placated. Besides, she seemed more amused than anything.

I'll soon put a stop to that.

"And what are you smirking about?" He struggled to focus. "Come to think of it…who the fuck *are* you?"

As Dave knew she would, Jane Barr tried to calm the situation. *That's my girl.*

"I invited her along. We met at my yoga class."

Dave leered at the new woman.

"Do you do contortions?"

The woman laughed.

"Well, I could tie *you* in knots."

She had a soft southern accent that Dave might even have found pleasant in other circumstances. He was about to reply but the drink had slowed him down by now, and the woman, Maggie, was already speaking across the table to Jane.

"When you said you'd introduce me to your friends, I thought you meant your sober ones."

Dave laughed, too long and too loudly.

"Nobody sober here except us chickens. We've all been drinkers, back since the first year at university, since Jane and I got together. Happy days."

Jim Barr butted in.

"There's your problem right there, Dave. All you do is talk about *the good old days*, and drink too much."

"They were the best days of my life," Dave replied.

"We were young, we were students, we drank a lot. Big fucking deal. What else is there to know? Move on. The rest of us have grown up," Jim said, his face getting red again. "It's well past time that you did, too."

Jane tugged at her husband's elbow, trying to stop him, but the argument had started to get heated, and the booze did Dave's talking for him.

"Grown up? Is that what you call it?"

Jim was in no mood to back down.

"You'd rather wallow in your own sad, little dream world? Look at the state of you. Get a life, Dave."

"I had a life...once." He looked at Jane, then back at Jim. "You took it away from me."

Jim sighed loudly.

"Not that old tune again, Dave. Give it a fucking rest. It's been nearly ten years...and it was your own fault. It's high time you faced it. You lost it. You had it all. Now look at you. Just another drunk with a grudge."

Dave stood, too fast, knocking over glasses.

"I might be drunk, but you're an uptight fucker with a pole up his ass. In the morning, I'll be sober. But that pole will still be there. You stole my life. And I want it back. I want what I deserve."

Glasses flew, tumbled and broke as he banged his fist on the table.

There was a sudden deathly silence.

All anger gone now, Jim spoke softly.

"Dave..."

"What is it now?" Dave said, still belligerent.

Jim pointed down to the table. Dave looked down to see a long cut on the outside of his hand where he had banged it down on broken glass. The drink had dulled his senses, but his sight was still good enough to spot the long sliver of glass still embedded in the wound.

Jane shouted.

"Don't..."

Without thinking, Dave pulled the sliver out.

"...take it out," Jane finished.

The wound gaped open. Blood spurted and mixed with spilled wine, creating a dark shadow that lay on the highly polished wood of the table.

Dave sat down, hard.

"Well, that was fun," he said. He had gone white, his eyelids fluttering.

Jim got up quickly and came around the table.

8

"Nice shooting, Tex. How bad is it?"

Dave held the hand away from his body. More thick drops of blood oozed onto the table. Jane also stood to come around the table. Dave waved her away, nearly knocking over another wine glass in the process and sending a spray of blood dots over one of the few white parts of the tablecloth.

"I'm OK. Don't fuss," he said.

Jane ignored him and turned to her husband. Just the sight of the look that passed between Jim and Jane made Dave's heart *lurch*, and suddenly all he wanted was more booze.

Lots more booze.

"The bandages are in the bathroom cabinet," Jane said to Jim. "I'll get them. Can you clean up here?"

Jim, suddenly sober, nodded and turned back to look at Dave.

"Try not to bleed on the carpet, Dave. If you remember, I've still got the mop pole up my ass."

Dave smiled wanly, and felt a well-recognized hint of shame for his inner turmoil.

Lots more booze.

Jim picked up the largest bits of glass from the table and left for the kitchen.

Dave held his arm up, studying the cut. Blood flowed down his arm, pooling in the rolled up sleeves of his shirt around the elbow. At the same time, Maggie leaned forward, taking a crystal pendant from around her neck.

"Here. Let me."

She started to run the crystal along the length of the cut. Dave took a while to focus, then pushed her away roughly.

"Hey! What do you think you're doing?"

"I'm using the healing energy of the crystal to rebalance your blood flow and…"

"Well you can stop that right now. I don't believe in any of that new age crap."

Maggie smiled.

"That doesn't matter. It's working anyway. Look. You've stopped bleeding."

Dave looked at his hand. The bleeding had indeed stopped. But he wasn't about to become a convert— not to this doe-eyed hippie.

"And the fact I'm holding my hand above my heart has nothing to do with it? Hello? Has no one else studied Biology 101 here?" He pushed her further away. "Healing crystals? It's a bloody rock. It has less healing energy than an aspirin. Do you want to stick some needles in me as well? Or maybe we can do some aromatherapy?"

"A better smell around here might be nice."

She was still smiling, and that just made Dave push harder.

"I'll tell you what. I'll fart, and you can tell me how I'm feeling."

The smile got wider.

"Bitter. Very bitter."

"Ho, ho. Very funny. Why don't you go and play in the garden? I'm sure there are plenty of trees needing a hug out there."

The smile finally slipped.

Got her!

"Jim was right," she said. "You need to ask the Cosmos for a life."

Jane came back in, carrying a small first aid box.

"I've been hearing about that recently…ask the Cosmos…what's that all about?" she asked Maggie.

Dave butted in before the woman could reply.

"Superstitious bullshit. That's what it is."

Jane held up a bandage.

"Are you going to play nice, or do we have to tie you up?"

I never could refuse her.

"Give me another drink and I'll be as good as a very good thing at obedience classes."

Jane started to bandage Dave's hand, grimacing at the mess.

"Come on, Maggie. Tell us about this *Cosmos* stuff. It'll take my mind off this," she said.

"If we're going to be listening to a load of old nonsense, I need a drink first." Dave shouted.

Jim returned, on cue, carrying a full bottle of whisky.

"Just one more. A nightcap," he said, and Dave smiled.

"You had the pole removed."

Jim smiled back.

"No. I'll need surgery for that. Thanks for reminding me."

"Hey. That's what friends are for."

Jim poured the drinks while Jane kept working on bandaging Dave up.

"Maggie?" she said. "You were going to tell us about the Cosmos thing?"

Maggie took a glass of whisky from Jim when offered, and took a long sip before replying.

"It's the latest thing in California."

Dave grunted, but a look from Jane quieted him fast as Maggie continued.

"It works on the principle that everything in the universe is connected."

Dave couldn't help himself.

"It's called Quantum Theory, darling."

Jane gave him a slap on the shoulder.

"We've listened to your crap all night, Dave. Give your ego a rest."

Anything for you, darling.

He went quiet and stared glumly into his drink as Maggie started to warm to the task. Her next question almost surprised Dave into sobriety.

"What do you see when you look at me?" she said. It took Dave a few seconds to realize she was talking to him.

"A hippie," Dave said. "And a delusional one at that."

11

"So I'm no more than a label? And that's it? What about a fellow human in pain?"

"Fellow human?" Dave said. "No such thing. We're all just information that needs a bit of tweaking."

"Information? What am I...Some kind of fucking computer?"

"Something like that," Dave said. He too was warming to the conversation now. It was taking a direction he could relate to.

"So you're a mechanist?" Maggie continued. "All human passion, all memory, all imagination...the complete human experience. All of it just comes from the chemistry in our brains...like the movements of a clock follow from the arrangement of its cogs and wheels?"

Dave nodded.

"Clockwork dolls, the lot of us."

"But who makes the dolls?"

"Why do you need a maker?"

"Why don't you need a maker?"

Dave laughed out loud.

"Any god capable of engineering all the organized complexity in the world must already be hugely complex in the first place. So arguing for the existence of a maker just moves the discussion back a step; you're still postulating organized complexity without offering an explanation. There's plenty of evidence that nature doesn't *need* an organizing principle. The basic laws of physics and chemistry are enough for life to find a way."

"A blind watchmaker?"

Dave nodded again.

"And what about love?"

Dave looked at Jane, then quickly away again.

"An anomaly brought about by the necessary complexity of the biochemical systems required to maintain our bodies."

"Now I see. You rationalize the pain you inflict with your bad attitude by seeing your victims as empty shells. To you, we are little more than sacks of shit and blood."

Dave waited to see if Jane would interject, stand up for him once more. But it seemed this time he was on his own.

"Now you're beginning to understand," he said.

Maggie looked at him, and he had to look away from the pity he saw in her eyes.

"I believe I am," she said. "And I believe I was right. You *do* need to ask the Cosmos for a life."

"Now we get to it," Dave said, taking a deep gulp of Scotch. "Bring out the trowels, there's bullshit to be spread."

Maggie sighed, but kept going, turning away from Dave and addressing herself to Jane.

"The theory goes that if you make a request to the universe in the right way, then the Cosmos will grant your wish."

Dave held his tongue this time, but it seemed the whisky had loosened Jim's.

"It pains me to say this," he said. "But I'm with Dave on this one. It sounds like more Californian BS claptrap to me."

Dave and Jim clinked their glasses together. Dave was about to say more, but was stopped again by a sharp glance from Jane. She finished bandaging his wound.

"There. All better."

Dave flexed the bandaged hand and smiled sheepishly. But Jane had already turned away to listen to Maggie.

"Never underestimate the power of the universe," Maggie said.

"Oh, I'm very careful around huge inanimate objects…they might fall on me," Dave said, earning him another of *those* looks from Jane.

At least she's noticing me.

"Maybe we should give it a go sometime?" Jane said.

Dave took a large gulp of whisky.

13

"To hell with sometime. There's no time like the present."

He turned to Maggie.

"What do we have to do?"

Maggie looked at Dave and smiled.

"It could be dangerous," she said.

There looked to be a hint of sadness in her eyes, and maybe condescension. That only served to push Dave into more taunts.

"It's put up or shut up time…or are you all mouth?"

Maggie looked across at Dave, and this time the anger was obvious.

"OK. Let's do it. Can I have some paper and pens please, Jane? And do you have four envelopes?"

While Jane was away, Dave and Jim helped each other to more of the whisky. Dave was getting a buzz on again, and the pain from his hand had dulled to a mild ache. He knew he'd pay for it in the morning.

But that's nothing new.

A minute later they all had pens and paper in front of them on the table.

Dave pretended to write while reciting *sotto voce*.

Dear Cosmos. Fuck off and die.

"Dave!"

That came from Jane.

"Live long and prosper?" Dave said, and Maggie laughed.

"Better. But that's still not couched properly." She paused and looked at the other three. "The thing to remember is that you should ask directly, say please, and ask for something you really want, something you have your mind set on."

Dave snorted.

"What a load of old crap."

Maggie looked about ready to take his head off.

"Just remind me. Whose idea was this?" she said.

The other three started writing. Dave stared at the blank paper.

"Tell me again…how is this supposed to work?"

Maggie began as if reciting something she'd read.

"The universe is more than just a collection of atoms. Advances in physics have proved that. A particle can also be a wave form, and Heisenberg showed us that the particle's state could be changed just by looking at it. Nothing can be observed without the observer having an influence. And that influence is what has created the universe that we perceive around us. In many ways it is a construct of our minds. The collective subconscious acts as a filter through which we create the consensual reality that we all experience. When we ask the Cosmos for a favor, we are really asking ourselves for a way to change our view of reality to one that is more favorable."

Dave laughed loudly.

"Ah, psychobabble. I recognize that. I remember when…"

Maggie's chair screeched on the floor as she pushed it backward in anger.

Dave laughed again. Jane put a hand on Maggie's arm and gently motioned her back into her chair before turning to Dave.

"Oh for God's sake, Dave, let's just get on with it."

Jane started writing again, tongue between her lips as she concentrated. Dave watched her then wrote.

"Please Cosmos, I want Jane Barr."

Jim leaned over and filled Dave's glass.

"Have some more, Dave. It's the one you got me for Christmas."

Dave looked, from Jane to Jim and back again. Disgusted with himself, he scratched out what he'd written, and replaced it with one sentence that he wrote so feverishly that his new bandage went from white to red and two fresh drops of blood fell to the paper to be incorporated into his handwriting.

Finished, he looked up to see that the others had also written their wishes.

"I'll show you mine if you'll show me yours?" he said to Jane.

Maggie was insistent.

"No. You mustn't let anyone else know. Fold your papers up, and put them in here." She gave each of them an envelope. "I'll pop them in a post box for us all."

They all did as she told them.

"Who do we address it to? Sanity Claus?" Dave said.

He left a smear of fresh blood on the envelope trying to get the sheaf of paper inside.

"No need," Maggie said, collecting the four envelopes. "The Cosmos knows where each needs to go." She checked her watch. "Speaking of which…I've got to be going too."

"Nonsense," Dave said, making for the whisky bottle. "The night is yet young…"

Jane spoke softly.

"It's half past one, Dave. Some of us need to get to work in the morning."

JUNE 11TH

I can't be doing with this *Twilight Zone* nonsense," the cop said.

Dave smiled.

"That's just about what I said. But let me show you something."

He put a hand in his shirt pocket. The cop flinched, and reached for where his gun would normally be.

"Relax," Dave said. "This is something by way of a demonstration, something Maggie showed me earlier, before…before…"

He couldn't finish the thought. Instead he took something from the pocket, a crystal hanging on the end of a chain.

"I'll try to remember all her exact words," he said. "It might be important…later."

He let the crystal hang on the end of the chain.

"Everything has a natural rhythm," he said. "The Earth spins once a day, goes around the sun once a year. The moon goes round the earth every 28 days. Your heart beats in a rhythm particular only to you. Everything has its drumbeat and everything contributes to the dance. You've just got to know when to lead and when to follow."

"I told you," the cop said. "No BS…"

Dave leaned over the table. The cop flinched again, but allowed Dave to let the crystal hang between them. It hung straight down, unmoving.

"Put your hand below it," Dave said. "Palm up. Come on. Humor me. It's all relevant."

The cop did as Dave asked.

The crystal started to move. First it swayed from side to side then slowly started to spin in a circle that widened until it rotated slowly above his hand.

"Take your hand away," Dave said.

Again the cop complied.

The crystal stopped moving and went back to hanging dead on the end of the chain.

"Now you try it," Dave said, handing the cop the chain.

The cop took the crystal and held it by the chain. The crystal hung dead until he put his hand under it, whereupon it immediately started to spin in a circle. When he took his hand away, the crystal went dead again.

The cop examined the crystal and the chain.

"Do you know what she said when I did that? *You're looking at the dancer rather than the dance.* Now, hold it over the water." Dave said.

The cop did as he was asked. The crystal swung in a much wider circle this time.

"Everything has a beat. Even water," Dave said.

"I think I've heard of this," the cop said. "It's dowsing, isn't it?"

Dave shook his head.

"Not quite. According to Maggie, a dowsing rod responds to electromagnetic fields. This is more of a mechanism for accessing innate rhythms. Your unconscious makes slight adjustments to your muscles in response to the rhythms, and these are amplified and turned into rotational movement by spin vectors being produced in your fingertips. The same as dowsing, but different, if you get my meaning?"

"This is just a stupid parlor trick. It has to be," the cop said. Even before he'd finished the sentence, the crystal started to move again, side to side at first, then settling down into a tight three-inch circle.

"That doesn't prove anything," the cop said.

"No. But it is *indicative* of something. It gives me hope, that there is more to life than just blood and flesh, that there might just be a point beyond staying alive as long as possible."

"I hope this is all leading somewhere, son," the cop said, handing the crystal back over the table. Dave put it away in his pocket.

"I just wanted you to understand how Maggie's mind works. It took me a while to get there myself, but it was worth it."

The cop sighed.

"More bullshit. I'm getting mighty tired of this."

Dave sat down in the chair, suddenly weary.

"Back to business then. I'm just telling you it as it happened. And that's how it went, that first night. I got drunk and made an ass of myself. Nothing new there. But that was how it all started," Dave said. "I heard on the grapevine that they'd done it all again with another couple of my friends, Frank and Liz, several days later. I hadn't been invited to that one…*persona non grata* and all that happy shit. But by the time June came around, I was forgiven and invited round to a barbecue. That's when things began to get seriously fucked up."

JUNE 5TH

D ave walked through a well-tended garden on a hot summer's day, heading for the back of the Barr's house. He carried a box of beer under one arm, and a bag containing two bottles of Scotch in the other hand. Even then he wasn't sure he'd brought enough booze to get him through the day.

He heard the sound of laughter coming from the patio at the side of the house, and almost turned and left. There were days when he wanted company for drinking. Today wasn't necessarily one of them. Then he thought of Jane.

I can't let her down. Not again.

He followed the sound of laughter. Jim Barr stood at the big gas cooker wearing a chef's apron; turning chunks of meat with a pair of tongs. The others, Jane, Frank and Liz, and Maggie, were all seated at a long table.

"We must stop meeting like this." Maggie said, sneering when she saw Dave walk up the path.

"Maybe it would be better if we just stopped meeting?" Dave replied. He'd had a few beers and a whisky stiffener before even leaving the house and was in no mood to be polite to an obvious nut job. But as ever, Jane was able to calm him down, at least to a semblance of politeness.

"Dave! Be good. Please?" was all she had to say.

Dave looked over at her, and softened slightly.

"OK. Just this once. But who is this woman, and why does she keep following me?"

"I told you last time…she's new in town…"

"So is Walmart, but you don't invite *it* over to lunch."

"Please, Dave? I thought she might be somebody you could talk to."

"I'll give her a mercy fuck if that's what she's after."

Jane was struck speechless, but Maggie laughed it off.

"I prefer my men to be capable of standing up…if you get my meaning?"

Jane giggled awkwardly, but Dave showed no sign of registering Maggie's remark.

"Who needs a beer?" he said.

The meal went the same way as most of Dave's recent lunches. They all had near-finished plates of food by the end, except for him. He hardly ate, but had a small forest of empty beer bottles in front of him. Once again, he was getting drunk twice as fast as anyone else at the table.

Jim and Jane sat close together, and he saw that Jane kept fondling the back of Jim's neck. Dave looked pointedly away, taking a long swig of beer. At the same time, Maggie moved her seat closer to Dave and leaned over towards him.

"So what do you do, Dave, out in the real world? When you're not getting smashed that is?"

Dave took another swig before answering, and when he did it came out too glib, as if it was a line he'd prepared earlier.

"I wheel shitty trolleys around shitty hospital corridors and watch good people die," he said, and the anger in his voice was evident. "But what's this about the *real* world? I thought you didn't believe in that?"

"What gave you that idea? My personal interface with the Cosmos is the realest thing I know."

"And what about the rest of us? Are we allowed to play as well, or is it all for you?"

Dave took another swig of beer. He was talking for the sake of it, not really interested. Maggie, however, seemed pleased to have at least got him listening.

"Do you know anything about Zen?" she asked.

It was Dave's turn to laugh.

"Only from re-runs of *Kung Fu*."

"Well, Grasshopper," Maggie said. "Everything is one, and one is everything."

"*I am he as you are he as you are me and we are all together?*" Dave said.

"Yes," Maggie replied. "We are the egg men. All together in one huge womb that is the Universe, the *macrocosm*. You mentioned quantum theory at dinner the last time. So you know already, all we are, all everything is, is energy and vibration, light and shadow."

Despite himself, Dave started to enjoy the conversation.

"I'll give you that one. Random acts among sub-atomic particles at the quantum level. That's what drives the Universe."

"And where we differ, is that I believe it's not so random," Maggie said. "In the same way that a magnifying glass can focus light into a spot that burns as bright as a sun, so the human brain can act as a lens, focusing emotion and will to create changes in its environment."

Dave laughed.

"That's just wishful thinking."

"In a way, yes, but it works. I've seen it."

"Like that shit we did last month?" He raised his voice so the rest of the group could hear. "How did that work out? Has the Cosmos been listening?"

No one replied so Dave plowed on.

"Come on, tell us. Has anybody won the lottery? Has anybody suddenly become handsome?" He turned to Liz. "I can guess what you asked for, Liz. Ready to pop one out yet?"

Jim waved a beer bottle towards Dave.

"Enough already, Dave. You're being a dick again."

"He's not even that interesting," Maggie said. "A girl could have some fun with a dick."

They all laughed, except for Dave

"At least I'm still rational," he said, too loudly, still letting the drink do his talking for him. "What about you lot? It looks like your Cosmos isn't listening."

Frank was the one to break the awkward silence.

"Well, that might not be strictly true," he said.

"And what might *that* mean?" Dave said sarcastically.

"Our envelopes came back," Liz said.

Dave's booze-addled brain refused to provide a witty comeback. It didn't look like anything he could say would phase Liz anyway. She was smiling broadly.

The cat that got the cream.

"We got the news this morning, right after we found that the Cosmos had replied."

Dave was too astonished to speak. He looked around to see if this was maybe all a practical joke they'd agreed to play on him before he turned up. But Frank too had a wide grin on his face.

"You tell them," he said to Liz.

Liz looked down and rubbed her belly.

"We're going to have a baby."

Again the booze made Dave speak without thinking.

"No fucking way."

Frank smiled.

"What other way is there?"

Jane stood and gave Liz a hug.

"I'm so happy for you both."

Liz looked across the table.

23

"We've got Maggie to thank. The Cosmos came through for us."

Dave stopped drinking his beer in mid-gulp.

"Now hold on a minute…"

"What else could it be?" Frank said.

"What else could it be?" Dave answered. "Did your I.Q. just drop sharply? What we have here is a coincidence. It can't be any more than that."

"A pretty big fucking coincidence, don't you think?" Frank said.

Liz put a hand on her husband's arm.

"God does not play dice with the universe," she said softly.

"Don't you dare quote Einstein at me," Dave said, his voice rising until he was nearly shouting. "Don't you dare."

Frank held up two white envelopes

"Then how do you explain these? They were on the kitchen table when we got up this morning."

"How the fuck should I know?" Dave said. He still had a beer bottle in his hand as he motioned towards Maggie. Beer slopped everywhere. "Why don't you ask the wicked witch of the west here? Or try asking the fucking Cosmos again."

Liz looked as if she was about to cry. Jim Barr had seen enough.

"Dave. You're being an asshole. Again."

Dave calmed down, but only slightly.

"I'm sorry, Liz. I'm happy for you. I really am. But this is your and Frank's doing. It's got nothing to do with a big fairy in the sky, and it's certainly not the Cosmos arranging your life for you. It's just good old rhythmic gymnastics and sperm and ovum."

Now it was Maggie's turn to get angry.

"How do you know? Come on, Dave, tell me, why are you so sure?"

Dave turned towards her.

"How do I know? I've got a fucking brain. That's how I know."

"I've got a brain too," Maggie started to say. Dave didn't give her time to finish.

"No. What *you've* got there is a cabbage. *I* don't need a fucking magic crystal to tell me where to find my ass."

Maggie looked him straight in the eye.

"Jim was right. You *are* a dick."

"And who the fuck are you to be saying that? You don't know me. You're just some cheap street magician who has conned Frank and Liz into thinking they're going to live happily ever after."

He turned to the couple.

"I'd watch out you two. It's only a matter of time before she asks you for money."

Maggie stood, knocking over her chair.

"Say that again," she said, softly.

Dave was too drunk to notice the fire in her eyes.

"Which bit? The bit where you're full of shit or the bit where you're a fucking evil bitch?"

Maggie stepped up to Dave and socked him in the jaw, hard. He'd had far too much booze to roll with the punch. He fell off his chair and landed on the grass in a crumpled heap.

Everything suddenly went quiet. Then Liz applauded, and Frank and Jane joined in. That, more than the ignominy of being knocked to the ground, made Dave feel about an inch tall.

Jim, smiling, looked down at Dave and offered him a hand to get up.

"Looks like the Cosmos knows your place in the scheme of things, Dave: flat on your ass and drunk as a skunk."

June 11th

"The next morning I woke with a hangover, and a phone call. It was you guys, telling me that Frank and Liz were dead," Dave said. He raised his head and looked the cop in the eye. "I never even got a chance to say goodbye. We never heard what caused the accident."

The cop spoke for the first time in a while.

"Accident? Oh, I doubt it was that. I doubt that *very* much."

He opened a file and took out a sheaf of pictures, laying them out on the table in front of Dave. They showed blown out tires, fused electrics, a smoking engine, and a vehicle with a front end that looked like it had run into a wall at high speed.

"The Connors' SUV ran into something else on the road that night. Something bigger and heavier than it; something that didn't hang around after the accident, something that left no trace at the site."

Dave stared silently at the pictures, horrified, as the cop continued.

"Let's go back a bit. After the woman knocked you down at the barbecue, what happened then?"

Dave smiled sadly at the memory.

"It put a damper on the party. I went home with my tail between my legs."

"No more was said between you and the Connors?"

"No. I never even said I was sorry."

"And you didn't take your car out for a spin later that day to try to give them a fright, just for a laugh?"

"No. I would never drive when I was drunk," Dave said, then stopped. Suddenly he could see where this was leading.

"Well, that's not really true, is it? I've seen your record," the cop said.

"What are you talking about?"

The cop opened a file on the table in front of him. The top page had Dave's mugshot on it.

"June, nine years ago," the officer said, tapping the page with his forefinger.

"That was an accident," Dave said, dismayed to hear the whine in his voice.

"You and I both know it was more than that, son," the cop said.

"I was young. And I was angry."

"No excuse then, and no excuse now. And the crash that killed the Connors' was no accident."

He put down a pair of pictures on the table. The dead, staring faces of Frank and Liz Connors looked up at Dave.

Dave looked back at them silently. It was a while before he spoke and then it was in a barely audible whisper.

"No. You're right. It wasn't an accident. Not this time."

He stopped and looked into the corner of the room.

"Did you see that?"

"There's nothing there, son. Quit stalling."

Dave started again, but didn't take his gaze off the corner.

"Have you ever had to bury a friend? It makes you have a look at yourself. And I didn't like what I was seeing."

June 10th

A small group of mourners filtered silently away as the funeral finished. The Barrs, Dave, and Maggie looked down at the twin grave where their friends had just been buried.

"Christine," Jane said, and started to sob. "They were going to call the baby Christine. Liz was so sure it was going to be a girl. She said that was what she'd asked for…"

She buried her face in Jim's shoulder.

"I never got to say sorry," Dave said. There was a hitch in his voice, and he was close to tears.

Maggie put a hand on his arm.

"Don't knock yourself out over it, Dave. There's nothing anyone could have done."

"I can't help it…They were so fucking happy. And I ruined it."

Jim Barr put an arm around Dave.

"Come away, Dave. Maggie's right. After you left the barbecue, Frank and Liz laughed it off. *Just Dave*, they said."

Dave didn't move, just stood, staring at the hole in the ground.

"Just Dave," he whispered. "Just Dave, being his usual dick self." He looked at Maggie. "If the Cosmos wanted somebody, it could have had me. I'm just about ready to go willingly."

Maggie led Dave away, a hand gently pressing on his back. He let her guide him as the four of them stepped away from the graveside.

"I need a drink," Dave said. For once, nobody disagreed with him.

They managed to find a table in a quiet bar.

Dave looked around and grimaced.

"Nice choice, guys. The last time I was in here was just before the accident. Remember? I wanted to get back to the hospital, but you all insisted I stay for another beer and…"

"That's not how I remember it," Jim Barr said. Dave waved him to silence.

"No. It wouldn't be. Then you'd have my life, and I'd have yours. And then…"

Jane leaned forward and put a finger to Dave's lips.

"Don't, Dave. Bringing all that up again won't help. Not tonight."

Jim passed Dave a fresh beer.

"Jane's right, Dave. Don't blame yourself for this. Let's just have a drink and remember Frank and Liz."

Dave looked like he might be about to get angry again, but Maggie put a hand on his arm and squeezed. He turned, she smiled, and from somewhere he managed to smile back.

Maybe I can get through this after all.

"Besides," Jane said. "Frank and Liz wouldn't want you to be angry. You know Frank. Mr. Compromise."

"Wherever he is, I hope he can find a fence to sit on," Dave said, and they all laughed, but there was little humor around the table and they soon lapsed into silence, lost in their own thoughts.

It was Maggie who spoke first.

"Isn't this supposed to be a wake?" She raised her glass. "To Frank and Liz."

Dave clinked his glass against hers.

"To Frank and Liz," he whispered.

Maggie seemed determined to lighten the mood.

"So who's got the best story? What's the most embarrassing thing that ever happened to Frank or Liz?" she said.

"Well, there was the time Frank walked in on Jim and I when he was drunk and tried to get into bed with us," Jane replied.

Jim laughed.

"He did that with his mum as well. It was…"

Dave finally broke into a grin. He put up his hand and snapped his fingers.

"I win."

He sat back, smiling.

"Go on then. Tell us." Maggie said, punching him in the arm.

Dave was now grinning widely.

"I can't. I promised Frank."

"Come on, you dick," Jim said. "Is it the stripper story?"

Dave milked the moment, taking his time over a sip of beer before replying.

"No. It's one even you haven't heard."

He shut up again and just sat there grinning.

Jane laughed.

"I suppose you'd better tell us then."

"OK, if you insist," he said, and paused again for effect until Maggie punched him, hard, on the arm. "It happened when we shared that dive of an apartment with no kitchen ceiling…Jim will remember that one well. The day Frank and I moved in we found a huge stash of porn under the floorboards…"

Minutes later all four were laughing fit to cry as Dave finished the story.

"So there's Frank, trousers round his ankles, and a huge erection standing to attention. And his mum says, calm as you like, *If you've finished with that tissue son, I need to blow my nose.*"

Jim laughed so much he snorted beer up his nose, and that set the other three off again.

"You should have asked the Cosmos for a TV show, Dave, that's the funniest thing I've heard in years," Jane said.

They all laughed again, but this time Maggie's laugh was a little less loud than the rest, and Dave noticed that she was now watching him closely.

Something changed, or I did something to change things. I wonder what?

The afternoon wore on, and the beer kept coming. They ate chips and burgers in the bar. For Dave it was just another reminder of better times, when they'd all used to meet regularly for lunches like this. Back then. Back before.

He was getting through the beers faster than the others, but so far had forced himself to wait until their glasses were empty before getting another round in. He knew it was only a matter of time before he hit the hard stuff.

All I have to do is wait. They'll leave. They always leave.

He was proven right in the early evening. Jim and Jane pleaded work in the morning and left. He expected Maggie to make her excuses at the same time, but she surprised him by not only staying, but by ordering another beer before Dave had finished his last one.

"Don't let me keep you," Dave said as she put two beers on the table. She laughed.

"Are you like this with every woman you meet, or are you making a special effort in my case?"

Dave was silent, staring into his beer.

"So, how did you all meet?" Maggie asked.

Suddenly Dave found that he wanted, needed to talk, needed to articulate some of the rage and despair that had gripped him over the days since Frank and Liz's deaths. He didn't look up, couldn't look Maggie in the eye, for fear of what he might see reflected there.

"We were all students at the same time. Jim and I go even further back. We came up through school together," he finally replied. He paused and took a long swig of beer. "I met Frank in a bar after a chess tournament and we shared a flat together. He met Liz on her first day at University, the first day of our second year, and they were inseparable ever since."

Although the bar was quiet and there were plenty of chairs, Maggie had moved to sit shoulder to shoulder with Dave, holding his arm. Dave found he didn't mind it a bit.

"I don't know what I'm going to do," he said. "Frank was the one who kept me alive after Jane and I, and after…"

He stopped. He was getting close to talking about the thing he wouldn't, couldn't, mention, the thing that remained securely locked in a dark place at the back of his mind. The thing he drank to forget.

Time to change the subject.

"Listen, I'm sorry about the thing at the barbecue," he said, finally looking up into Maggie's eyes.

She smiled and squeezed his arm.

"What, the *fucking fraudster bitch* thing? I already got you back for that one."

Dave rubbed at his jaw and smiled wryly.

"Maybe you did at that," he said. "It was just that I wouldn't believe. It goes against everything I know. I was such an asshole know-all that I upset them. And that's the last time I'll ever see them. This Cosmos of yours is one sick fucker."

"I don't think it cares," Maggie said, softly. She touched the back of his hand and started to stroke it. "Let it be. You heard Jim. Frank and Liz didn't hold anything against you. And neither do I. Besides, I've got a confession to make. I was at that dinner party under false pretenses. It's true that Jane asked me. But she did it because she thought I might be able to talk to you."

"Talk to me about what?"

"Anything you like. That's what I do. I'm a therapist."

"You're a small turtle?"

Maggie laughed, and Dave realized he didn't mind that either. He didn't mind it at all.

"I help people," Maggie continued. "But it would be all a bit too New-Wave and Californian for you. I realized that straight after meeting you."

"And how about now? What's the prognosis, doc?"

Maggie smiled again

"I need more time. But let's get saying goodbye to Frank and Liz over with first."

Dave looked down into his drink for a long time before speaking.

"Frank was *so* worried that they wouldn't be able to conceive. I had to get him drunk before he'd tell me. He was blaming himself, afraid that he was firing blanks."

A light wind seemed to blow across the table, ruffling Dave's hair. There was a hum in the air, like an engine idling in the distance. Dave didn't notice, too engrossed in his own thoughts.

"Getting pregnant was all Liz ever wanted. They'd been trying for years; Frank gave me a running commentary every time we met for a beer. I know more than I'll ever need to about the optimal temperature inside a pair of jockey shorts and how to calculate ovulation cycles, or how to optimize orgasms for maximum reproductive efficiency.

"Then along came this *Cosmos* thing, and *bingo*, they've got a bun in the oven. Liz was so happy at that barbecue. And I had to go and be an asshole about it."

Maggie took his hand in hers and held it gently. The breeze faded to nothing, and a new song kicked in on the jukebox, replacing the sound of the idling engine. Tears rolled down Dave's face, but he didn't take his hand away...and Maggie showed no sign of letting go.

———————

After the bar shut, they made their way by cab to Dave's flat where the drinking continued. Dave, if he'd been on his own, would have dived straight into the whisky bottle, but with Maggie there, he made do with wine.

"Come on, Dave. Tell me. There's something bothering you," Maggie said. They were sitting side by side on a sofa. Dave had gone quiet again, almost sullen. He drank quickly, finishing a large glass of wine in one gulp and pouring himself another. He laughed hollowly, but didn't reply, just took another swig of wine.

Maggie pressed on.

"It's to do with your question, isn't it? I saw the look on your face when Jane mentioned it."

Dave sighed heavily.

"It's just all this *Cosmos* shit. I can't believe there's anything in it."

"But you're starting to wonder?" Maggie said quietly.

Dave nodded.

"Now I'm starting to wonder. I'm starting to wonder whether I got my friends killed."

"What do you mean?"

"Remember," Dave said defensively. "I was drunk when I wrote it. Drunk and angry."

"You were angry with Jim all right. What did you wish...that he really did have a pole up his ass?"

"I could handle that," Dave said.

Maggie laughed loudly, trying to lighten the mood. "Whoaa! There's an image I don't need in my mind."

She didn't even get a smile in reply. Dave was lost in his thoughts, staring blankly at the wall opposite them.

"Frank and Liz are dead. And it's all my fault," he said, barely above a whisper. "That stupid fucking note I wrote to the Cosmos."

"What did you ask for?" Maggie said.

"I can't remember the exact words. But it was something about taking us away from everything to save us from our own stupidity."

Maggie got to her feet, agitated.

"And you got your envelope back. Didn't you?"

Dave looked sheepish.

"I found it in my pocket when I got back from Jim and Jane's. I had a sore jaw, I needed more booze, and I figured you'd planted it on me, to teach me *another* lesson. I ripped it up into little bits and threw it away."

"What did you do with the bits?"

Dave kept drinking, pouring the last glass from the bottle.

"They're in the waste paper bin. Or rather they were. I put it out this morning and…"

But Maggie had already left, hurrying out of the door.

He found her out in the alley between the buildings going through the garbage skips.

"You'll never find anything," he said. "There's five families with kids sharing here. There's always a huge pile of bags."

Maggie ignored him, raking through the bags, tossing garbage out of the skip into the alleyway.

"I'm not going to be popular," Dave said, dancing back to avoid being hit by something wet and rancid.

Maggie paused, hands full of lettuce and vegetable peelings.

"It's a bit late now to be worrying about that, isn't it? Now get up here and give me a hand."

"What's so important?" Dave said, clambering into the skip and realizing, too late, that he was still wearing his best suit trousers and shoes that he'd worn to the funeral earlier. Maggie seemed to have no qualms about getting her own clothing soiled. She was knee-deep in garbage, already stained with a variety of kitchen waste products. Undeterred, she kept digging.

"I need to know what you asked for," she said. "Exactly what you asked for."

They scrambled around in the rubbish, tearing open bags and sifting the contents. Dave stuck his hand on a cold, half-eaten, slice of pizza.

"Tell me again why we're doing this?" he said, trying to wipe the goop off his hand onto a piece of paper that was already slightly slimy, coated with something Dave didn't particularly want to think about too closely.

"I've already said," Maggie replied, not stopping her scrambling amid newly opened bags. "We need to know exactly what you asked for."

"Why?"

She stopped what she was doing and looked Dave in the eye.

She's scared stiff.

For the first time, he started to feel a tingle of fear himself.

"I need to know how bad it's going to get," Maggie said, and went back to the search. Dave looked down at the pile of garbage bags beneath him, thought of the booze waiting for him back in his apartment, then saw that Maggie's efforts had got even more frantic.

I may be a shit, but even I draw the line at leaving a woman alone to go through garbage in an alley.

He bent and tried to help. They sifted almost every bag in the skip over the next twenty minutes. Every time they opened a new bag a fresh batch of noxious smells hung around them.

We're going to stink for a week.

Dave had almost reached the end of his tether when he pulled open what he had vowed would be the last bag...and saw a torn piece from a white envelope. There was a smudge of red on the corner.

From when my wound oozed blood from the bandage.

"I think I've found a bit," he said.

"Good. Hold on to it. Is there more?"

Dave looked down. There were a lot of small pieces of paper among the rubbish under his hands.

"Most of it I think."

He bent for a closer look.

A wind ran through the alleyway, threatening to disperse the scraps of paper. The noise of an engine started up, but there was no sign of a vehicle in the alley.

"Maggie? Did you hear that?"

Maggie looked around.

The wind got stronger, the hum of the engine louder.

"Oh shit," Maggie said. "I think we're in big trouble." She bent to lift the scraps of paper Dave had found and stuffed them in her pockets. "Get as much of it as you can. And be quick."

The wind started to howl through the alley. Garbage was picked up and swirled everywhere around them. The noise of the engine revving rose until it was almost deafening.

"Have we got it all?" Maggie shouted.

Dave couldn't take his eyes off the swirling garbage; it danced, like a small tornado whirling and spinning through the alley. Paper and rotting vegetables were sucked into the vortex. It grew larger, noisier, ever more violent with each passing second.

Maggie grabbed Dave by the shoulder and turned him to face her.

"Have we got all of the fucking thing?"

The profanity finally shocked Dave into action. He looked down. There was no trace of any white paper below him. While he was checking, a layer of frost ran over the garbage underfoot. He felt cold creep through the thin soles of his shoes. His breath steamed as the temperature suddenly plummeted. The revving engine echoed loudly in the alleyway, like a kid getting ready to race a hotrod away from the lights.

Full-beam headlights swept the alley from side to side, although there was no apparent source of origin. The engine revved even louder, contending with the whistle and roar of the still growing wind.

Dave was rooted to the spot.

I've heard that same sound before.

"Time to go." Maggie shouted. Without waiting for Dave, she jumped out of the skip. Dave followed but landed awkwardly, his left foot sliding on some rotting vegetables, sending him falling, off-balance to the ground.

The engine roared louder, like a lion sensing a faltering prey.

Maggie grabbed Dave's hand and dragged him to his feet. Headlights washed over the alley, throwing huge black shadows on the walls to loom menacingly above them.

"We need to get out of here. Right now," Maggie said.

The engine revved behind them as they fled, the noise seemingly chasing them down the alleyway. It was only when they reached the main street that the noise started to lessen.

"Where are we going?" Dave asked.

"Anywhere that's not here," Maggie replied.

Behind them the wind dropped as quickly as it had come and the garbage fell in a heap to the ground. The alleyway fell silent except for the hum of an idling engine.

JUNE 11TH

The cop looked at Dave and raised an eyebrow.

"If you're planning on trying for an insanity plea," he said. "You'll need to come up with something a bit more creative."

Just as Dave was about to reply an engine revved nearby. Dave jumped and started to rise, thinking of heading for the door.

"Sit down, lad," the cop said. "You're not going anywhere until I can make some sense of all of this."

Dave sat still, listening. There was no repeat of the engine noise. He allowed himself to relax slightly, and laughed bitterly.

"It's sense that you want, is it? I think you're going to be sorely disappointed. It's all downhill from here. Things got seriously weird almost as soon as we got to Maggie's place."

JUNE 10TH

They finally caught a cab four blocks away from Dave's place. For almost half an hour they'd jumped at every shadow, cringed at every engine noise. Even after they were inside the cab, Dave didn't feel safe; the shadows seemed to gather and creep around him, and he was sure if he just listened hard enough that he would hear the whistling and roaring of the wind.

Maggie kept hold of his hand throughout the ten minute cab ride to her place, and after she let go to pay the driver, he quickly grabbed hold again as they walked up the short driveway to her house.

"I need to get my key," she said. "So you'll have to let go. But I promise you, we can hold hands as much as you like once we get inside."

She smiled, but Dave couldn't muster one in return. He was thinking of booze again. An ocean of the stuff, enough so that he could lose himself.

And the Cosmos can go to hell.

Maggie showed Dave through the front door, along a hallway and into a room full of New-Age paraphernalia; every available space was filled with crystals, dream-catchers, scented candles, and incense.

This time Dave managed a smile.

"Don't tell me. Your parents lived in a camper van and your real name is Galadriel Moonchild?"

Maggie grinned in return.

"Actually, my dad was an accountant. But we don't have time for *Ask the Family*. Phone Jane and Jim. Get them over here."

She gathered crystals from a display cupboard while Dave stood in the center of the room, bemused.

"It's going on midnight. They'll be in bed."

"Then wake them. In case you haven't noticed, we are in serious trouble here, Dave."

"I don't understand," Dave said. His mind was full of the sound of a revving engine, the dazzle of headlights that appeared out of nowhere. He wondered whether the drinking had finally caught up with him.

Maybe this is what they mean by 'delirium tremens'.

Maggie pointed him to where her phone sat on a table by the sofa.

"I'll try to explain if I get a chance," she said. "But I'm going to be busy for a few minutes. Just make the fucking call, Dave."

Dave moved to the phone. He paused before dialing.

"What do I tell them?"

An engine noise filled the room and Maggie stiffened, but it was just a car passing in the road outside.

"Tell them anything you like. As long as it gets them here fast."

Dave dialed the number from memory. Jane answered on the second ring.

"Sorry, Jane. It's me," Dave said.

"Do you know what time it is?" she said. She sounded bleary, barely awake. Dave heard Jim shout, as if in the distance.

"It's Dave again, isn't it? What's he fucked up this time?"

Just about everything, by the look of things.

"Sorry, Jane," Dave said again. "I need a favor. A big one."

"Can't it wait till morning?"

"I'm afraid not. Maggie says it's important. It's about the Cosmos."

"Come on, Dave. You of all people wouldn't wake us up for that."

"I don't have time to argue, Jane. Please? Can you and Jim get over here to Maggie's place?"

"What, now?"

Dave heard Jim shout again.

"Tell him to fuck off. I've got work in the morning."

"Please Jane? For me?"

Dave hung up the phone and turned to see that Maggie had set up some crystals in two concentric circles on the floor.

"Are they coming?" she asked.

"Jane will. But Jim…"

He made a see-sawing action with his hand.

Jane and Jim stood in the hallway of their house. Jane pulled on an outside coat. Jim stood, coat in hand, showing no sign of putting it on.

"Tell me again why I've got to drive out to the sticks in the middle of the night."

"Dave said…"

"Oh yes. Fucking Dave. What does he want this time? Let me guess. He's fucked his life up again?"

"He says it's important."

"When he's drunk, everything's important."

"He didn't sound drunk."

"Well, that'll be a first then."

Jim started to put on his coat. A white envelope fell out of a pocket. He bent to pick it up, then realized what it was.

"How did this get here?" he said.

"I've no idea. Is it what I think it is?"

"Fucking hocus-pocus, that's what it is. Wait a minute. It's not about this crap, is it?"

Jane put her hands up defensively.

"Dave said…"

"Can we please forget about Dave for a second?"

He waved the envelope in her face.

"Please tell me it's not about this crap?"

"He said that Maggie thought it was important."

"So it *is* about this crap. I've had enough. I'm going back to bed."

He tore the envelope up and let the pieces flutter to the ground. As the first piece hit the floor, the light bulbs in the overhead fitting all blew at once with a fizzle and pop.

"Oh for fuck's sake," Jim said, loudly. "That's *all* I need."

Everything fell quiet, then from nowhere yet everywhere a wind blew through the room. The noise of an engine started up.

"Jim?" Jane said, more than a hint of fear in her voice.

"It's just the fuse panel."

The room went icy cold, frost running across the carpet. The wind rose to a near gale. As if from nowhere, bright light flooded the room, and just as quickly cut off.

The Barrs fled, rushing outside, heading for the SUV in the driveway. The noise of an engine revving filled their house as they drove off in a screech of tires.

The sound of the SUV receded into the distance, but engine noise continued to run in the empty house before it was finally cut off and silence fell.

JUNE 11TH

The cop interrupted Dave's story.

"Wait. How do you know what happened after you phoned them. You weren't there."

Dave shook his head.

"I don't. I'm just guessing, based on what a dick I was to them over the years, and what I know happened to them on the way to Maggie's place."

"But it *was* you who called them from the house in the country?" the cop asked.

"I said that already, didn't I?"

"I'd just like you to confirm, for the record, that you invited the Barrs to that house."

Dave sighed.

"OK. For the record. It was me that invited the Barrs to that house. Happy now?"

"Not yet. But some pieces are starting to fit together. Tread carefully from here on in, Mr. Burns…you're getting to the bit I'm interested in."

"That's what I'm worried about. You're never going to believe me."

JUNE 10TH

M aggie motioned Dave over to the two concentric circles of crystals on the floor. She stepped over, into the inner circle, and held out her hand.

"In here. Quick."

Dave looked down.

"What is this? Magic hour?"

Maggie held her hand out again.

"We don't have time for twenty questions. It's coming. And don't ask what. You've already experienced it. Are you going to give me grief over this?"

Dave took her hand and stepped into the circle. He motioned at the crystals at their feet.

"OK, I'm here. Now, please, tell me what this is for?"

Now that she had Dave where she wanted him, Maggie seemed to relax slightly.

"The crystals act to focus my mind, to give us protection against whatever that was that nearly got us in the alley."

They stood there side-by-side in the quiet semi-darkness.

"I've been meaning to ask you about that," Dave said.

Maggie squeezed Dave's hand, gently.

"I told you on the night this all started. I don't know a lot about how the *Ask the Cosmos* principle is supposed to work."

Dave squeezed back.

"Smart move that, getting your excuses in early."

Maggie gave him a weak smile back.

"But I believe it's happened because of the strong emotions around the table that night," she said.

"Emotions can't affect reality."

"Why not? Yours have been affecting your reality for years."

That hit home, and Dave came to the realization that maybe, just maybe, the fault had been his all along.

"That's different," he said. But in his heart, he knew she had got straight to the nub of the matter.

"Is it Dave? Is it really?" Maggie said. She held his hand tighter. "Looks like we're not going anywhere in a hurry. Let's see if we can get to the bottom of what *really* happened that night at the dinner party. Tell me about the accident, Dave."

"How do you know about that?"

"I only know the fact that you had one. And that it's important."

"Oh, it's important all right. But maybe not in the way you think. Before it, I was in charge of my own destiny. I was a smart medical student, on the way to a good degree."

"And Jane? Where does she come in to this story?"

"She doesn't. Jane and I had already split up by then. There's a whole other tale to be told there, of friends lost, and jealousy causing me to push away the only good thing that had ever happened to me. But that's not what you need to hear tonight."

Dave looked Maggie in the eye.

How much do I tell her? How open do I want the wound to be?

"I was drinking, but I had it under control, mostly, except for when I had to see Jim and Jane together. Then they invited me out for a beer." Dave stopped, and had to brush away sudden tears. "I spent a long, miserable afternoon, watching them together. I so wanted her to be happy. But I wanted her to be happy with me, not him. So I drank, more than I should have. Then they made me stay for another beer, after I was ready to go."

Maggie looked about ready to say something, then changed her mind. She saw that Dave was lost in a time far away.

"It wasn't the beer anyway, it was an accident waiting to happen," he said. "It was a bad night. The wind howled like a banshee. Then the snow came down. I never even saw what I hit."

He stopped talking. Fresh tears ran down his cheeks. Maggie gripped his hand tight, but kept quiet. Dave was about to say something when she put a finger to his lips.

"It's starting," she said, quietly.

A wash of light ran across the ceiling.

Dave whispered. "I'm not sure I like this very much."

A cold wind blew through the room. An engine revved, twice, then fell silent. Dave remembered to breathe. They stood there holding hands for several minutes, neither of them speaking.

Eventually, Dave whispered again.

"Is that it?"

As if in answer, the temperature plummeted. A web of frost crawled across the inside of the windows with an audible crackle. Maggie's hair blew in Dave's face as a wind gusted out of nowhere. The engine noise revved louder, an impatient driver just waiting for the signal to accelerate.

Maggie pulled Dave close and spoke into his ear.

"Keep inside the circle. We should be safe here."

"Should be, or will be?"

By now frost covered all the surface of the windows, so thick it looked almost opaque. The noise of the engine revving up sounded as if it came from right beside them. The wind whistled, sending their hair flying, tugging at their clothes. The floor froze underfoot, cold biting into Dave's feet and ankles. A twin beam of headlights ran around the walls.

As quickly as it had started, it stopped. Everything went completely silent again.

Maggie and Dave looked at each other, fear in both their eyes, their breath steaming in the air, their skin pale, almost blue from the cold.

A loud bang came from the front of the house. Maggie started to move but Dave tightened his grip on her hand, keeping her close to him.

"It could be a trick," he said.

The noise was repeated. The banging became more frantic.

"Dave?"

It's Jim.

Dave started to move. This time Maggie pushed *him* backwards.

"Don't leave the circle. I'll go."

She let go of his hand and stepped out of the circle. She stood, just outside Dave's reach, and waited to see if an attack would come. Nothing happened.

Jim Barr banged hard on the front door again. Maggie went out into the hall beyond and now Dave could only see her as a dark silhouette. Beyond her there was a darker shadow looming outside the front door.

"Is everything OK?" Dave shouted.

"Shush!" Maggie replied in a mock whisper.

Renewed thumping on the front door caused Maggie to jump again.

"For fuck's sake, Dave. Let us in. It's coming back."

Maggie relented and opened the door. Jim Barr stood there, holding up an unconscious, bleeding Jane. Even as the door opened, Jim started to fall. Maggie got to him just in time. With Jim half-carrying Jane, and Maggie trying to support all three, they staggered towards the main room.

Dave started to step out of the circle.

"No. Stay there," Maggie shouted. "I've got this."

She pushed Jim and Jane into the circle. Jane's trailing leg caught some of the crystals, sending them rolling across the hardwood boards.

Wind blew through the room. An engine, impossibly loud, revved up. Light washed across the walls.

"Take them," Maggie said to Dave. "I've got to complete the circle."

Dave nearly fell over as he took charge of the combined weight of Jim and Jane. Jim crumpled, exhausted, to the floor, taking Jane down with him as Maggie moved to fix the gap. She had to step outside the protection to fetch the last two crystals. The engine howled in anger, and the wind buffeted her, threatening to knock her sideways. She forced her way against it, stepped back into the circle and placed the crystals on the floor.

The room fell quiet and still once more. The only sound was Jim's labored breathing.

"What happened?" Dave said.

Jim looked up, tears in his eyes.

"Wind, lights, noise…it all happened so fast. I never even saw what I hit."

June 11th

The cop interrupted Dave again.

"Wait a minute. You're saying it was all the fault of some noise and wind?"

Dave nodded wearily.

"I told you that you wouldn't believe me."

"You were right. You're going to need more than just a good lawyer, son," the cop said. "You're going to need a miracle. And as for all of this noise and wind...where is it now?"

"I don't know."

"And that's going to be your defense, is it?" the cop asked, putting on a sing-song, childish voice. "It wasn't me. A big invisible thing did it and ran away."

An engine revved up nearby, and a shadow ran around the walls of the interview room. Dave flinched, but the noise wasn't repeated. He sat back in the too-small chair and sighed.

"If you liked that, then you'll love the rest of it."

June 10th

Jane bled from a head wound. Jim was bent over her, trying to coax her into opening her eyes.

"Is she OK?" Dave asked.

Jim looked up, his own eyes full of tears.

"We need to get her to a doctor, Dave. She won't talk to me."

Dave turned to Maggie. She was about to answer when the wind blew through the room. All the lights in the house came on at once. They brightened, casting harsh shadows as the light got more and more intense, until, finally the bulbs blew in a series of small explosions. Electric sparks ran across the light switches. Something hissed, and suddenly there was smoke in the air and an acrid taste in Dave's mouth as all the cabling in the walls burned.

The room went dark. Smoke from the burnt cabling drifted, like fog, across the ceiling above. An engine revved, almost deafening in the small room.

"What the fuck is happening here?" Jim said.

Silence fell. Dave heard his heart beat in his ears, three thumps before the engine revved again, accelerating through the gears. The wind blew a gale, so strong that Dave felt it tug at him, threatening to lift him off his feet. Maggie grabbed him by the arm, and they braced themselves against each other.

Headlight glare filled the room, then just as quickly switched off.

Everything fell silent again.

It's playing with us.

Maggie and Dave stared at each other. He saw his own fear in her eyes.

"We have to get out of here," Dave said.

Maggie shook her head. "It's too dangerous. Look what it did to Jane."

Dave looked down, just in time to see Jane's eyes flutter and rolled up to show the whites. She went limp in Jim's arms.

Jim shook her, shouting.

"Jane. Stay with me. Jane!"

Maggie bent next to him and gently tried to move him aside.

"Let me see her, Jim."

Jim looked up at Dave.

"What can I do? What can I do?"

"Let Maggie have a look. Come on…"

Dave put out a hand. Jim laid Jane down gently and took the offered hand. Dave lifted him to a standing position as Maggie bent down and checked Jane. After what seemed like an age, she looked up.

"She's alive, but out cold."

Jim tried to pull away from Dave.

"I'll get a doctor."

Around them, the room fell deathly quiet as if waiting, expectant as Jim's foot raised to step out of the circles. Dave pulled him back.

"No, Jim. Don't break the circle."

"Don't break the circle? I don't give a flying fuck about any circle. That's Jane lying there. She needs a doctor."

He pulled free from Dave…and stepped beyond the outer circle of crystals. In his haste, he kicked a section of the crystals. They scattered, some shattering against the skirting board, others rolling off into dark corners.

A wind rode up, howling, as if in triumph.

Frost crawled across Jim's body.

The engine screamed as it revved up to top throttle.

Headlights spun around the room, faster, almost strobe-like.

Dave moved to help, but Maggie was already bent over, repairing the circle of crystals with those she could reach. She put a hand on his thigh, holding him back.

"No, Dave. It's too late."

Dave tried anyway. He started to leave the circle…just as Jim was struck by a force so strong that he flew across the room as if hit by a truck. His body hit the far wall with a sickening crash and fell to the floor, contorted and broken. He didn't make another sound, didn't move.

The wind dropped. A cooling engine ticked over and then was cut off. The wash of light dimmed and faded until they were left in darkness. The room fell completely silent.

Maggie and Dave stared at each other again, dumbstruck.

Jim Barr's body lay lifeless on the floor, staring straight at Dave.

————————

It was a long night.

When dawn finally came, Dave was sitting on the floor with Jane cradled in his arms. Maggie stood over them. The frost melted away from the main windows and sun streamed in. An engine started up, revved once, then faded away into the distance. A cool breeze seemed to pass over the defensive circles then everything was once again still.

Jane's eyes fluttered. When she spoke, blood bubbled at her lips.

"Jim? Put the light on, Jim. It's too dark."

"It's me, Jane. It's Dave."

"Jim? Is that you? Turn the heating up. I'm cold. Jim? Did you hear me?"

Dave looked up at Maggie, tears in his eyes.

"What do I do?"

"Just hold her. That's all you can do."

"Jim was right. She needs a doctor."

"We can't risk leaving the circle."

Jim's body remained against the wall, staring at them, a reminder of that fact.

"Jim? Where are you?" Jane said. She sounded weak, barely able to speak above a whisper.

"I'm here," Dave said.

"I love you, Jim," she said, her eyes fluttering, breath coming in hot gasps.

"I love you too, sweetheart," Dave said, tears blinding him

Jane stopped breathing, dead eyes staring.

It was some time later before Dave laid Jane's body down and stood beside Maggie. His eyes were hard and cold as he took her hand.

"OK. I'm a believer. How do we beat this thing?"

"I don't know. But I think I know where to find out."

"Come on then. Let's end this."

He stepped out of the circle. Maggie followed, still holding his hand as they stood, waiting. Nothing happened.

"I guess the cosmos is busy elsewhere," Dave said bitterly.

He led Maggie out of the room. As he closed the door behind them, he turned for one last look at the bodies. They both had an arm outstretched. It looked as though they were reaching for each other.

Dave closed the door gently behind him.

JUNE 11TH

The cop snorted.

"So you admit it then. You fled the scene?"

Dave laughed.

"Yes. We fled. We were fugitives from justice. Running all the way to the nearest library. Was it really just this morning?"

JUNE 11TH

M aggie got a battered VW Beetle out of her garage and drove them to the University library, an old Colonial building that Dave hadn't been in since his own student days many years earlier. And back then, he certainly hadn't been perusing the stacks for books like the ones Maggie piled on the desk.

The Mysteries of the Wurm, On Ye Philosophie of Life and *A Treastise on Death.*

He picked up the latest one she'd fetched and read the inside cover.

Ye Twelve Concordances of ye Red Serpent. In which is succinctly and methodically handled, the stone of ye philosophers, his excellent effectes and admirable vertues; and, the better to attaine to the originall and true meanes of perfection, inriched with Figures representing the proper colors to lyfe as they successively appere in the practice.

"Some light reading then?" Dave said, but Maggie had her serious, no nonsense look working for her. She sat down opposite him and started taking notes, switching often between several of the books in front of her. Dave sat quietly and watched her work.

At some point he fell into a fitful sleep filled with dark dreams of revving engines, whistling wind, blind panic and fear.

He woke with a start to find Maggie shaking him. On looking around, he saw that everybody else in the library had turned to look at him.

"You screamed," Maggie said.

"Are you surprised?"

She didn't answer, just helped him out of the chair.

"I think I've got what we came for," she said.

"OK. What now?"

"Now you take me home…your home."

"Best offer I've had all year," he said, but neither of them was much in the mood for jollity. They drove to Dave's apartment in silence.

———————————

Maggie didn't give him time to settle once they got inside.

"We've got a spell to prepare," she said.

"You see, this is where we have a problem. Normally, I don't hear that said very often."

Maggie had already sat down at the kitchen table and was again scribbling furiously in a notebook. Dave started making coffee. When he went for the cups, he found a nearly full whisky bottle in the cupboard beside them. He took it down and unscrewed the top. He looked over at Maggie, her head down in the notebook. He screwed the top back on and put the bottle back in the cupboard.

Maggie smiled when he handed her the coffee.

"You didn't put any stiffener in it then?"

"Maybe later," Dave said. "After we get the Cosmos sorted out."

Maggie sat upright, stretched and flexed her neck.

"I think I've got it now," she said.

"So can it be done?"

"If this is right, yes, we can."

Dave sat down opposite her.

"Tell me."

She ran a hand through her hair.

"I told you about focusing of the will?"

"Yep. But…"

"No buts, Dave. Not now. That night, when we sent the Cosmos our messages, you were angry."

"I had every right to be, I…"

"Dave. Shut the fuck up."

Dave thought about arguing, but part of him already knew he had lost the fight. He let her talk.

"You were so angry, and had so much focus, that you've bent reality to your own will, created something out of your subconscious to fulfill your purpose. And you have to be the one to get rid of it."

Dave put down his coffee.

"Then let's have at it. What do we do?"

"What, no argument about what a load of crap it all is?"

"Not any more."

Maggie finished off her coffee.

"We can't do it here. It has to be back at the Barr's house…back where it started."

Dave went pale.

"I'm not sure I can go back there yet. Not after Jane. After she…"

He couldn't finish the sentence, and struggled to hold back fresh tears. Maggie stood, came around the table and hugged him from behind.

"It's the only way," she said. "Otherwise it won't stop until the original intent is fulfilled. My guess is that you'll be left till last…and that means I'm next."

It was approaching dusk again by the time they arrived at the Barr's place. Dave opened the door, slowly, carefully, as if afraid what might be behind it. The hallway was dimly lit by streetlights outside, but dark shadows sat like pools in the corners. Dave eyed them warily. He tried a light switch in the hall. Nothing happened.

Maggie joined him in the hallway, and shut the front door behind them.

"Jane had plenty of candles that night at the dinner party," she said. "Let's try the kitchen."

The kitchen, being at the back of the house, lay deeper in darkness than the other rooms, and it took what little courage Dave could muster to make him walk inside. He rummaged, half-blind, in the cabinet drawers and finally came up with some candles and a box of matches.

"Found them!"

He lit a candle. It flickered and sputtered alarmingly, casting dancing shadows across the walls that only served to remind him of the manifestations they had seen the night before.

"That's much better," he said sarcastically.

Maggie gave him a thin smile. She held up a small pile of white envelopes and patted him on the shoulder as she walked past him. She picked up the candle and headed for the dining room.

"Let's get this done."

They sat down on opposite side of the candlelit table.

"What now?" Dave said.

Maggie took out the pocketful of scraps she had collected in the alleyway outside Dave's apartment. Seeing what she was doing, Dave did the same. When they were done, a small pile of rubbish sat on the table between them.

"We need to find as much as we can of the original message," Maggie said. She lifted up some small scraps of paper and let them fall. "How are you with jigsaws?"

It took over an hour, but finally Dave was able to look down on a patchwork piece of paper held together by tape. There were some pieces missing, but the gist of it could be read.

Dear Cosmos. Please take us away from all of this crap.

Maggie read it from over his shoulder. "Yep. That sounds like you all right."

"That was all it took?" Dave said, whispering.

"That, and the right circumstances, in the right place and time."

Dave read the note again, then looked at Maggie.

"What do I have to do."

"Let's see if we can confuse the Cosmos and get it to change its mind."

Maggie handed Dave an envelope, paper and pen.

"Reverse the spell. Just don't let me know what you're writing. And while we're at it, I'll do one too…let's call it some insurance."

Dave wrote.

Dear Cosmos, OK, I get the message. Please leave me alone now.

He looked up to see Maggie staring across the table at him.

"Finished?" she said.

Dave nodded.

"What did you ask for this time?" he said.

Maggie shook her head.

"I can't tell you that," she said. She put the messages in the white envelopes and sealed them. "Now, we wait."

They stood up from the table. As he moved his chair back, Dave saw a shadow shift in the corner. He put a hand on the table. It felt cold to the touch, and getting colder.

"I think we're in trouble."

Maggie blew out a forced breath. It condensed in the air in front of her face, only to be quickly dispersed as a wind blew through the room. An engine revved up. Headlight beams crossed the room slowly.

Maggie dropped the envelopes on the table and pushed Dave towards the door.

"Run!"

Wind and engine noise filled the room. Maggie and Dave fled, heading for the front door. Dave threw it open…and nearly knocked over a cop who had his hand raised, ready to knock.

"Sorry, can't stop," Dave said, and pushed past the startled officer. With Maggie's hand still firmly in his, they ran down the street, expecting a shot to follow at any second. The cop gave chase. Police sirens wailed in the distance, and when Dave chanced a look around he saw that two cops now followed them, some distance behind.

The wind howled in their ears.

"I thought you said it would be over?"

Maggie struggled for breath.

"Not until the Cosmos answers. We need to get our envelopes back first."

The running policemen were catching them quickly. Even as Dave looked for an escape route, two squad cars screeched to a halt beside them. Cops got out, guns were pointed at them. Dave and Maggie stopped running. They had nowhere to go.

"I hope you asked for something that'll come in useful in the long years we'll be spending inside," Dave said as his hands were pulled roughly behind his back to be cuffed.

Maggie half-smiled as they were led into separate police cars.

"I'll see you later."

The wind howled up several notches, then died to a whisper.

An engine revved, then fell silent.

June 12th

"That's it?" the cop said. "It's past midnight, we've been at this for hours, and *that's* your story?"

Dave nodded.

"And what about these?

The cop threw three white envelopes on the desk.

"Three?"

"Two from the Barr's house, and one from the coat of the deceased, Jane Barr. I take it these are your *requests to the Cosmos*?"

Dave nodded again.

"And now that you've got them back, if your story is to be believed, it should be all over?" the cop said.

"That's the theory."

"And a pat one at that. All very convenient. Your friends all die and no one gets the blame?"

"I've told you. It was my fault. I asked the Cosmos."

"And nobody will believe it, will they? Once more, all very convenient for you. But then again, you've got a history, haven't you?"

"What do you mean?"

"Tell me about the accident, son," the cop said softly.

"The accident? What does that have to do with anything?"

The cop picked up one of the envelopes, opened it, and read.

Dear Cosmos. Please let Dave admit the real cause of the accident to himself.

"She wrote that? Maggie wrote that? I hardly know her. And she hardly knows me."

"Maybe so, but it wasn't her doing. Mrs. Barr wrote this one."

"Jane? No. She wouldn't."

"But she did," the cop said. "And now she's dead. So, once more for the cheap seats, tell me about the accident, son."

"It wasn't my fault," Dave said, almost shouting.

"Change the record, that one's getting tired."

Dave put his head in his hands.

"It wasn't my fault," he said again, but even as he spoke he knew he sounded like he was trying to convince not only the cop, but himself.

"OK. We'll get back to that," the cop said. "But first, let's see what *you* asked the cosmos for." He opened one of the two remaining envelopes.

Dear Cosmos, I get the message. Please leave me alone now.

He looked over at Dave.

"*Please leave me alone.* Not, *please leave us alone,* not, *please stop killing my friends.* That tells me all I need to know about you."

"I loved her," Dave said.

"Who? Jane Barr? No, you didn't. You blamed her, didn't you? Blamed them all for everything." He patted Dave's file on the table in front of him. "You blamed them, for the crash, for having to quit med school, for the drinking, and for the shitty jobs you've been doing ever since. You blamed them all. And it ate away at you so much, year after shitty miserable year, until you finally cracked and you killed them, so that you wouldn't have to look at them anymore."

"That's not how it was." Dave said, his voice rising into a shout. "It was the Cosmos."

"And tell me, how does the Cosmos manifest itself? But you've already told me that. It sounds like a car, an engine howling on a cold windy night."

The cop paused and looked Dave in the eye.

"Tell me about the accident, son.

––––––––––––––––––––

Dave wasn't sure what he was going to say until he opened his mouth. When he started to talk it was little more than a whisper.

"I didn't realize how much I'd drank. And everything happened so fast. It was a really shitty night, I was driving too fast, an angry drunk raging at the world. I wound the window down, the wind ruffled my hair and whistled in my ears, joining the roaring of the engine as the only things I could hear.

"And then suddenly there she was. A young girl. She stepped in front of the car, eyes wide in terror."

Dave stopped and looked up at the cop, tears rolling down his cheeks.

"She was right in front of me. I couldn't get out of her way."

"You killed her," the cop said baldly. "She was just ten years old. And you blamed everybody but yourself. You still do."

Dave shook his head.

"There's nobody left to blame. Just me. And the Cosmos."

"But you said already. The Cosmos has done its thing. It's finished. Now there's only you."

"Only me," Dave whispered.

A wind whistled through the room in reply.

"It was only ever me."

A car engine revved up.

"It wasn't the Cosmos."

Headlights with no apparent source swept through the room. The cop had time for three words. "What the fuck?" An invisible force threw him across the room to land in a still, crumpled heap against the wall.

"No," Dave shouted. "It was finished."

Blood poured from the cop's head and pooled on the floor. Dave immediately had a flashback to the night it all started, and to the too-red blood pooling on the Barr's dining room table.

"It was only ever me," he whispered.

He headed for the interview room door, calling Maggie's name. As he reached it, a young cop opened it from the outside. Before the cop could speak, the wind whistled, an engine revved up and the young officer flew, screaming, down the length of the corridor to smash, headfirst into a wall. Headlights washed the scene.

"Maggie!" Dave shouted.

The wind rose to a howl, the engine revving alongside it. Lights washed the corridor, strobe-fast.

"Maggie!" he shouted again. A door opened and she stood there, eyes wide, wind tossing her hair in a mane around her head. Dave almost fell into the room beside her, pushed in by the force of the wind.

"It was me all along," he shouted, struggling to be heard.

"I don't understand. We undid it," Maggie shouted back.

"No. It wasn't the Cosmos. It was me. All this time it was me."

He lifted a water glass from the table and smashed it against the wall.

"Back at the dinner party. I wasn't angry when I wrote to the Cosmos. I was angry when I banged the table. Remember?"

You stole my life, you bastards. And I want it back. I want what I deserve!

Glasses fly, tumble and break as he bangs his fist on the table.

Blood pools.

The noise of the engine howled through the room. Ice ran across the windows. The headlights washed around the room, faster and faster.

Dave dropped a large piece of glass on the table.

"It was my years of self-pity, blaming the people around the table, the police, anybody but myself. All that despair, focused into a moment's rage. That is what we have to undo… what *I* have to undo."

He raised his fist.

"No!" Maggie shouted, and put a hand on his arm before he could bring it down on the table.

"You don't understand, Maggie," Dave said. "I blamed everybody around the table…including you. You have to let me do this."

He pushed her away and raised his fist again.

"No, Dave. Don't!"

Dave banged his fist down on the table.

"It was all my fault. I want what I deserve."

A shard of glass went deep into the old wound. He pulled the glass out, and blood pooled on the table.

"It was all my fault," Dave shouted.

The wind rose to a wailing gale, an engine revved. Something struck Dave so hard that he flew across the room, hitting the wall. Maggie ran to his side. He was barely conscious. She knelt beside him and took his head in her lap.

Dave coughed, bubbles of blood at his mouth.

"Looks like the Cosmos was listening this time."

Maggie tried to smile.

"It always is."

Dave looked up at her, straining to focus.

"You never told me what you asked for."

"Do I have to?"

She kissed him, lightly. The wind died down. The headlights went out. The engine revved, once, then fell silent. When she looked up again he was dead, eyes staring blankly from a smiling face. She closed his eyes, tenderly.

About the Author

William Meikle is a Scottish writer, now living in Canada, with over thirty novels published in the genre press and more than 300 short story credits in thirteen countries. He has books available from a variety of publishers including Dark Regions Press and Severed Press and his work has appeared in a large number of professional anthologies and magazines. He lives in Newfoundland with whales, bald eagles and icebergs for company. When he's not writing he drinks beer, plays guitar, and dreams of fortune and glory.

BIBLIOGRAPHY

<u>NOVELS</u>
The Green and The Black / Crossroad Press
The Boathouse / Crossroad Press
Ramskull / Crossroad Press
Songs of Dreaming Gods / Crossroad Press
The Dunfield Terror / Crossroad Press
Fungoid / Crossroad Press
The Hole / Crossroad Press
The Exiled / Crossroad Press
Night of the Wendigo / Crossroad Press
The Ravine / Dark Regions Press
The Invasion / Dark Regions Press
The Valley / Dark Regions Press
The Creeping Kelp / Dark Regions Press
Crustaceans / Dark Regions Press
Sherlock Holmes: The Dreaming Man / Gryphonwood Press
Berserker / Gryphonwood Press
The Midnight Eye Files: The Amulet / Gryphonwood Press
The Midnight Eye Files: The Sirens / Gryphonwood Press

The Midnight Eye Files: The Skin Game / Gryphonwood Press
The Concordances of the Red Serpent / Gryphonwood Press
Watchers: The Coming of the King / Gryphonwood Press
Watchers: The Battle for the Throne / Gryphonwood Press
Watchers: Culloden / Gryphonwood Press
Watchers: Omnibus edition / Gryphonwood Press
Eldren: The Book of the Dark / Gryphonwood Press
Island Life / Gryphonwood Press
The Road Hole Bunker Mystery - Charade Media

NOVELLAS
Operation: North Pole / Severed Press
Operation: Orkney / Severed Press
Operation: Patagonia / Severed Press
Operation: London / Severed Press
Operation: Sahara / Severed Press
Operation: Yukon / Severed Press
Operation: North Sea / Severed Press
Operation: Congo / Severed Press
Operation: Mongolia / Severed Press
Operation: Norway / Severed Press
Operation: Syria / Severed Press
Operation: Loch Ness / Severed Press
Operation: Amazon / Severed Press
Operation: Siberia/ Severed Press
Operation: Antarctica / Severed Press
Infestation / Severed Press
The Lost Valley / Severed Press
Sea Hunters: Shonisaurus / Severed Press
The Land Below / Severed Press
The Sea Below / Severed Press
The City Below / Severed Press
Tormentor / Crossroad Press
Clockwork Dolls / Crossroad Press

Sigils and Totems: A Collection of Novellas / Crossroad Press
Broken Sigil / Crossroad Press
Pentacle / Crossroad Press
The Job / Crossroad Press
The House on the Moor / Dark Regions Press
The Plasm / Dark Regions Press
Professor Challenger: The Island of Terror / Dark Regions Press
Sherlock Holmes: Revenant / Dark Regions Press

SHORT STORY COLLECTIONS
Inspector Lestrade: The Black Temple / Weird House Press
The Ghost Club / Crystal Lake Publishing
Dark Melodies / Dark Regions Press
Carnacki: Heaven and Hell / Dark Regions Press
Carnacki: The Watcher at the Gate / Dark Regions Press
Carnacki: The Edinburgh Townhouse / Lovecraft ezine
Carnacki: Starry Wisdom / Dark Regions Press
Sherlock Holmes: The Quality of Mercy / Dark Regions Press
Professor Challenger: The Kew Growths / Dark Regions Press
The Midnight Eye Files: Omnibus / Gryphonwood Press
The Midnight Eye Files: Omnibus 2 / Gryphonwood Press
Samurai and Other Stories / Crystal Lake Publishing
Myth and Monsters / KnightWatch Press

Curious about other Crossroad Press books? Stop by our
website: http://crossroadpress.com
We offer quality writing
in digital, audio, and print formats.

Subscribe to our newsletter on the website homepage and receive
a free eBook.